For Liv Isabel Victoria

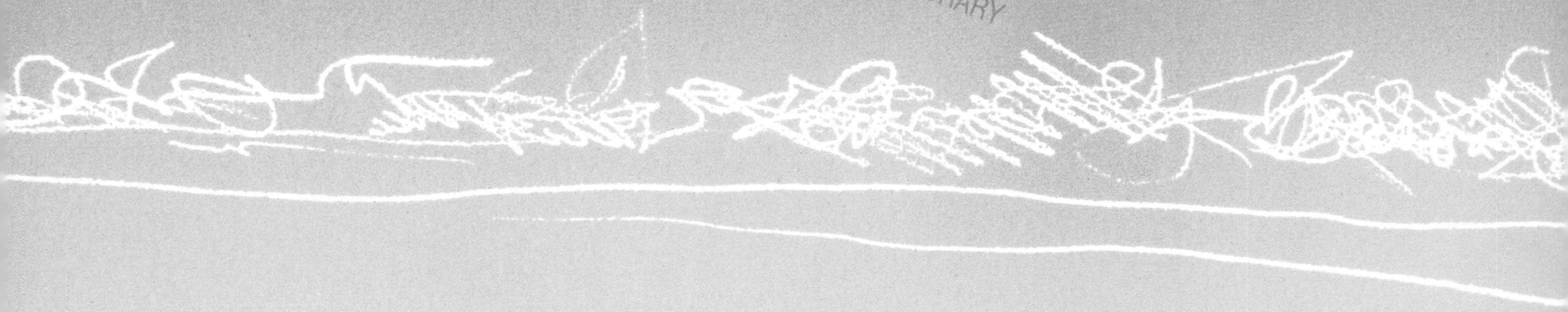

# the island

Marije Tolman & Ronald Tolman

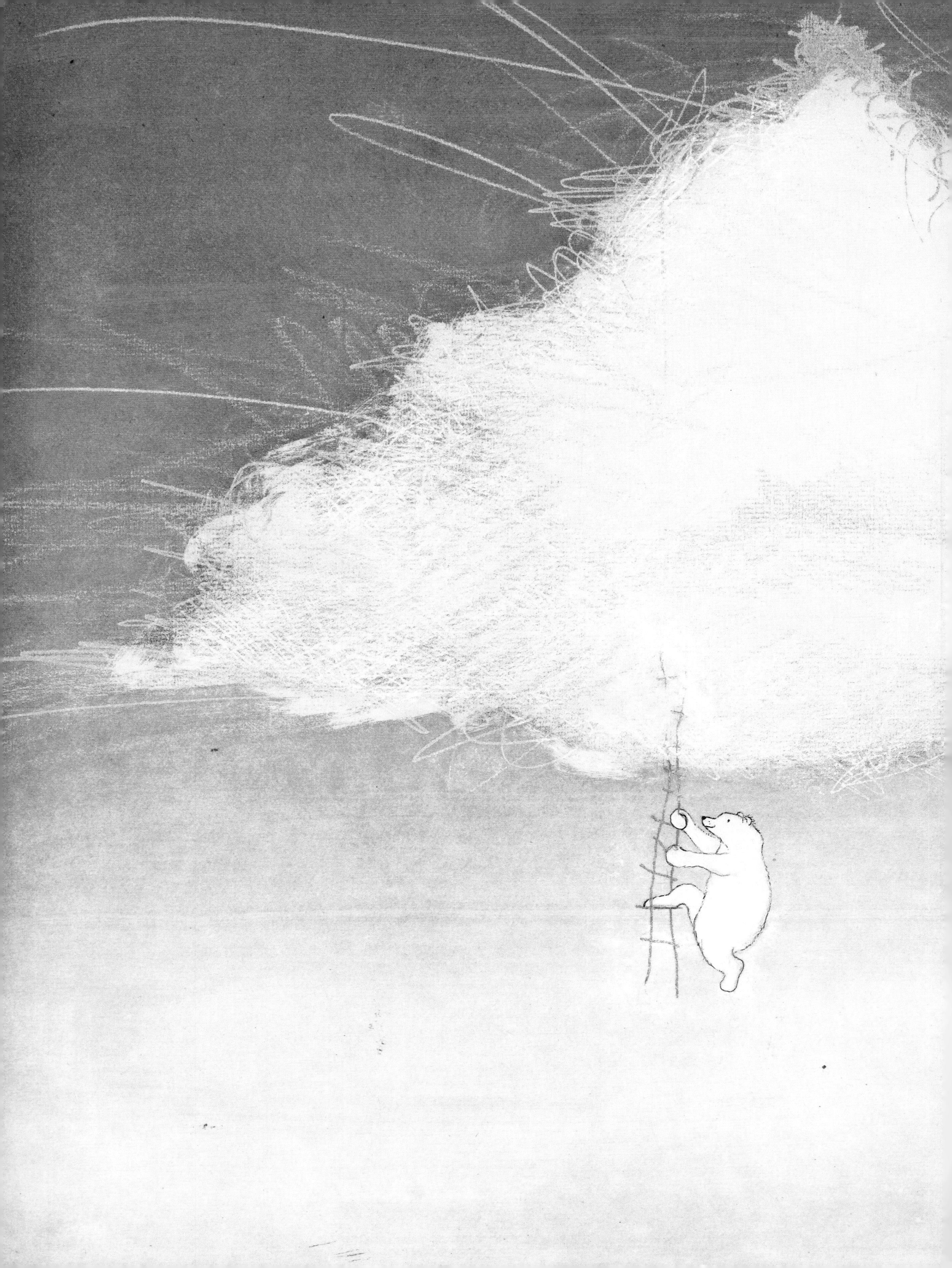

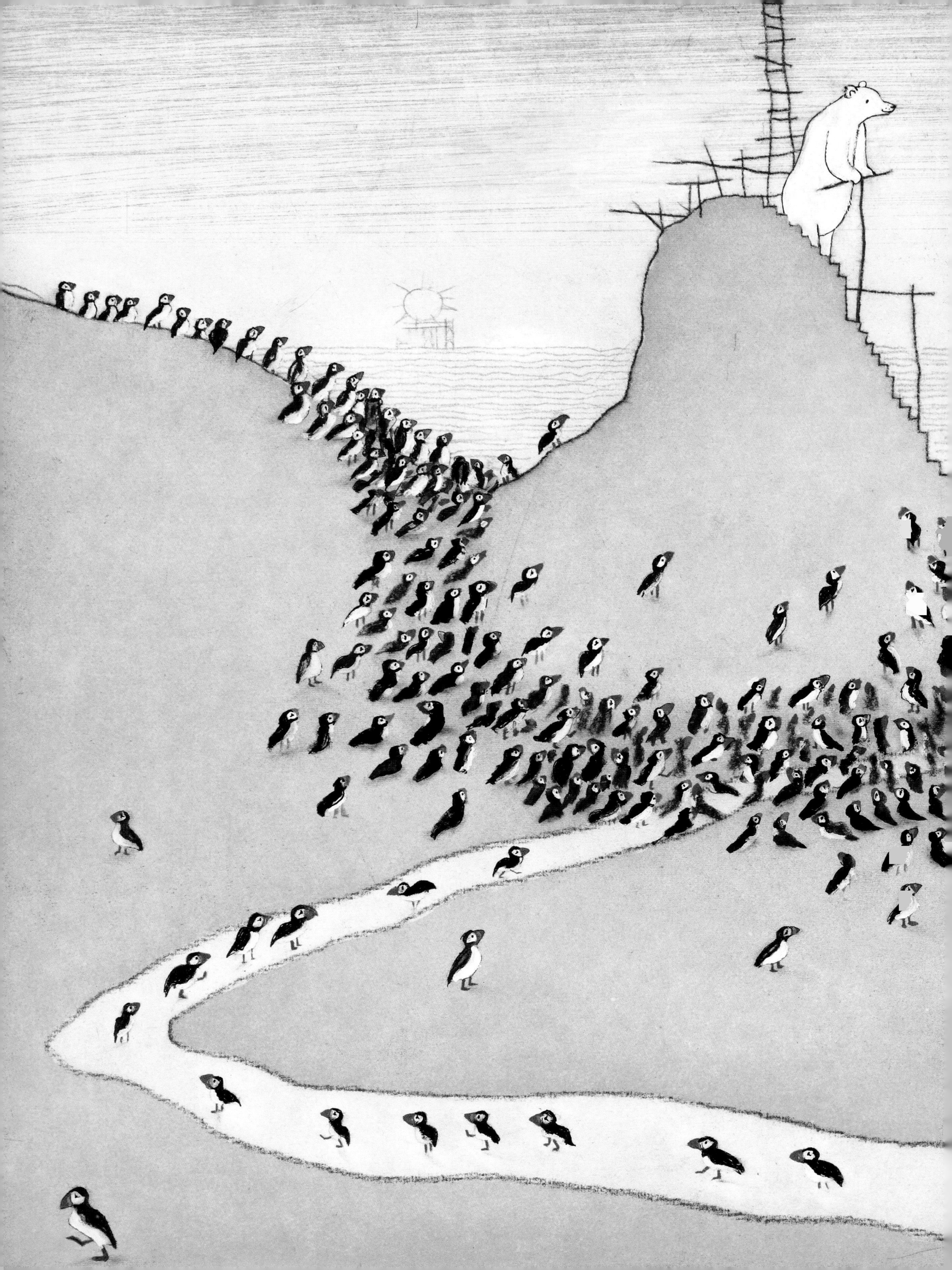

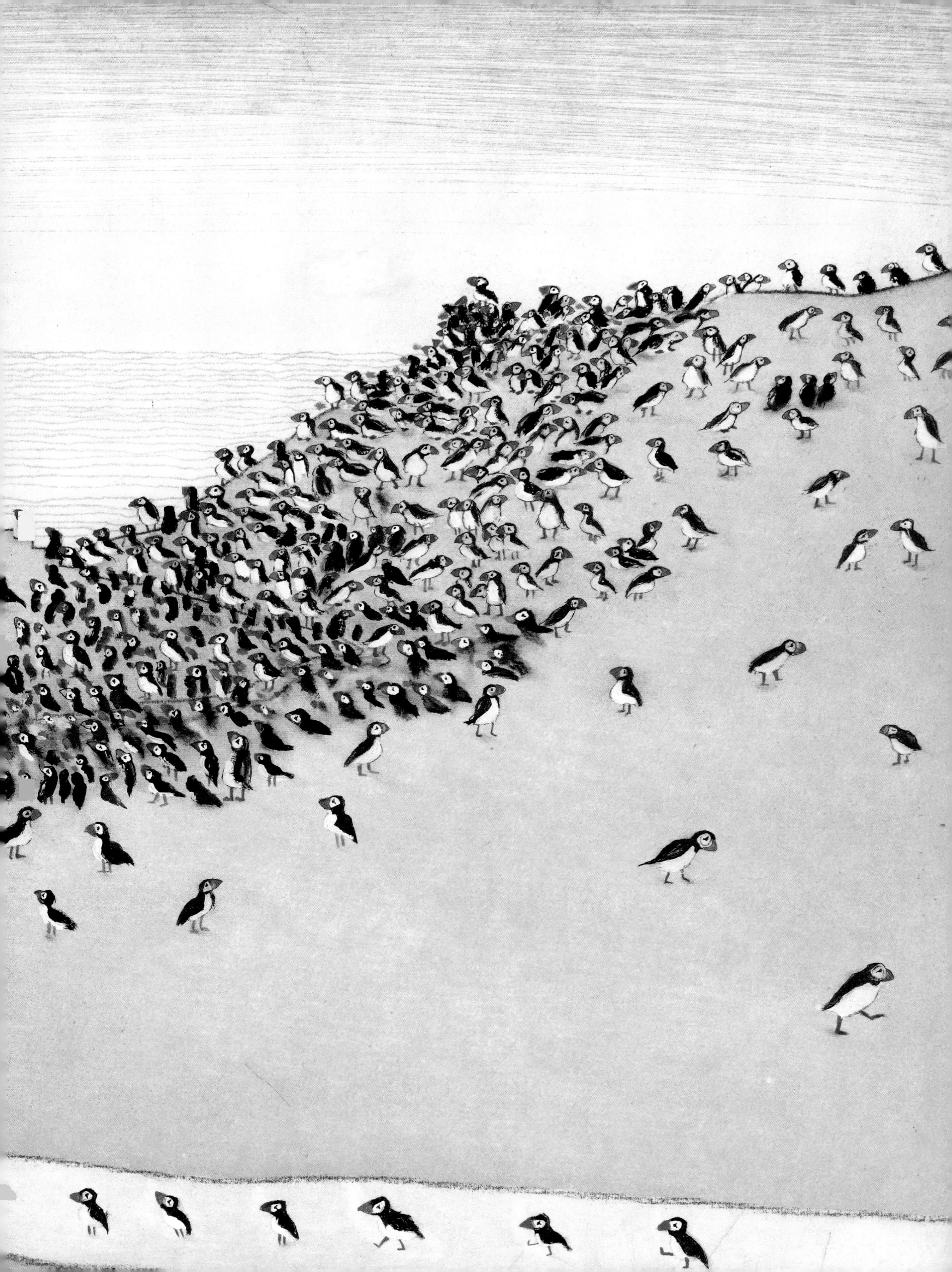

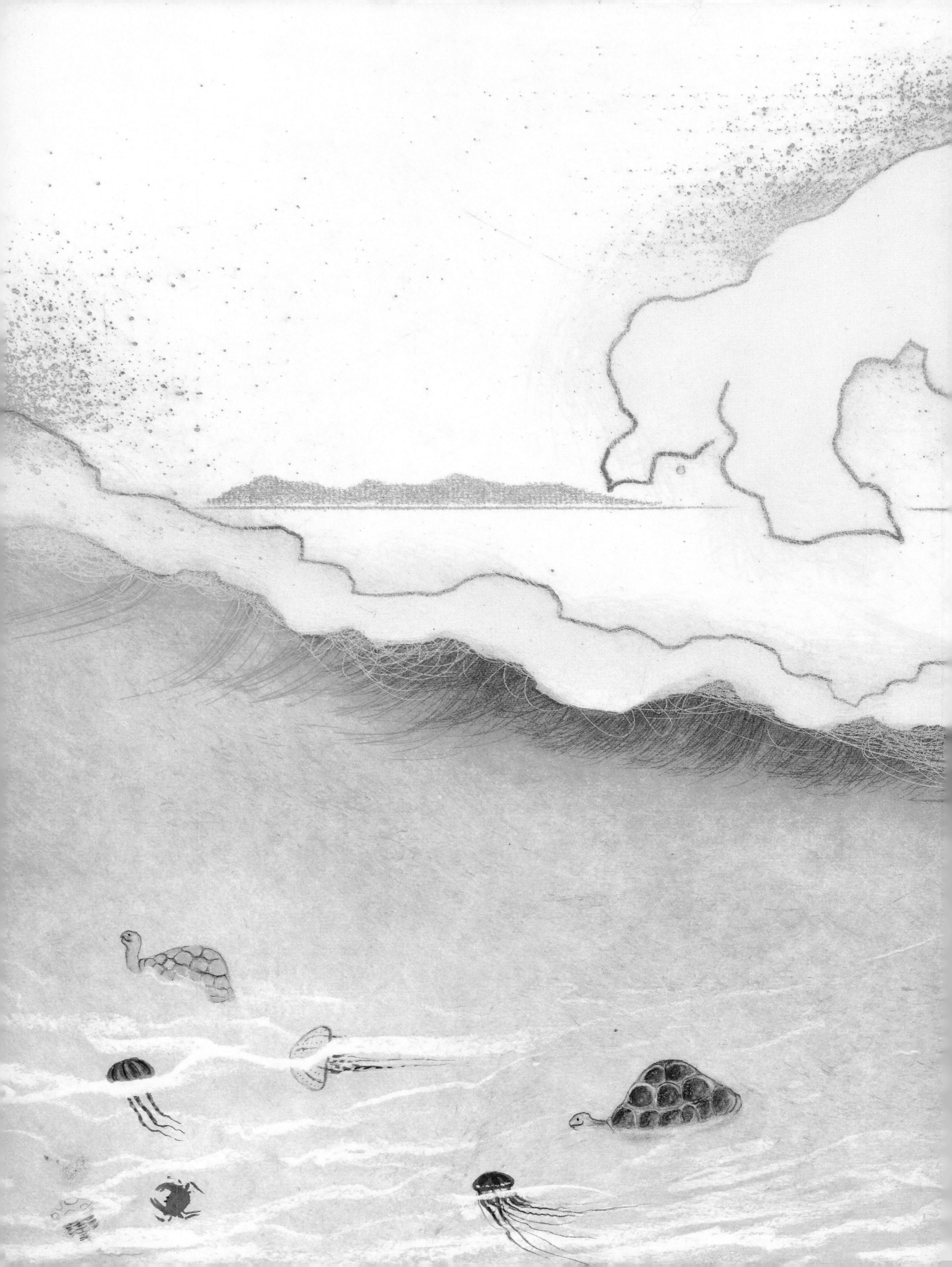

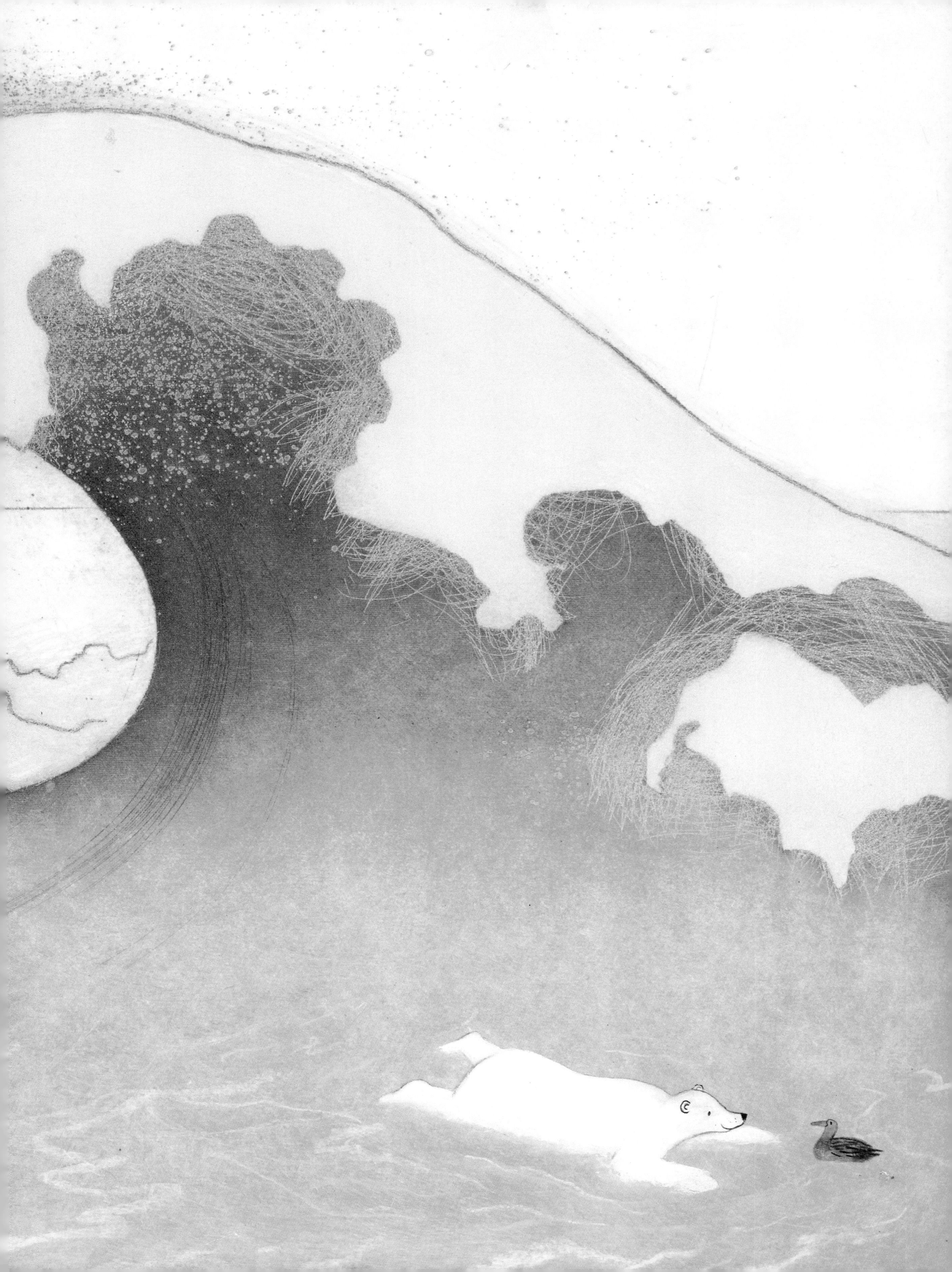

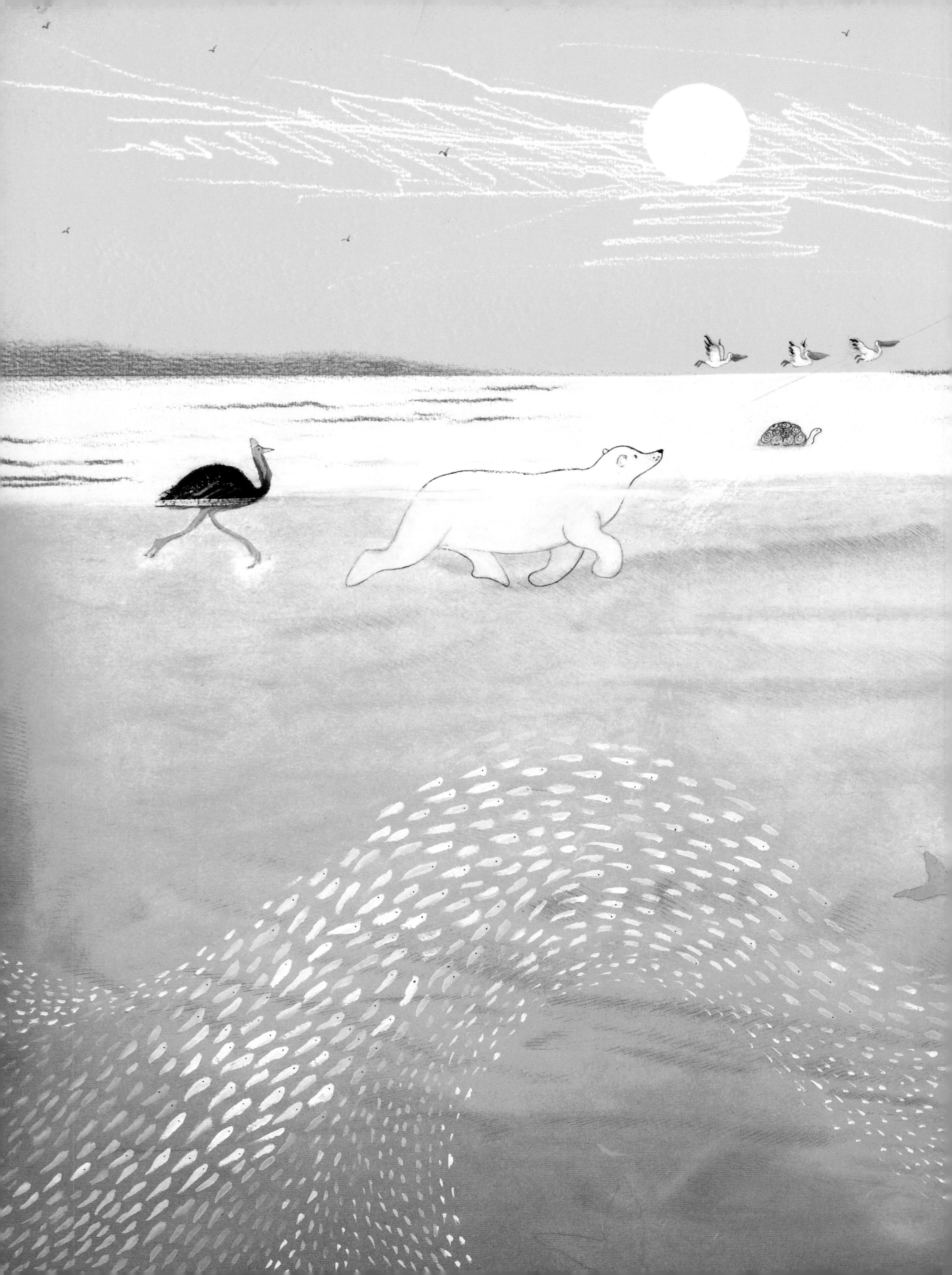

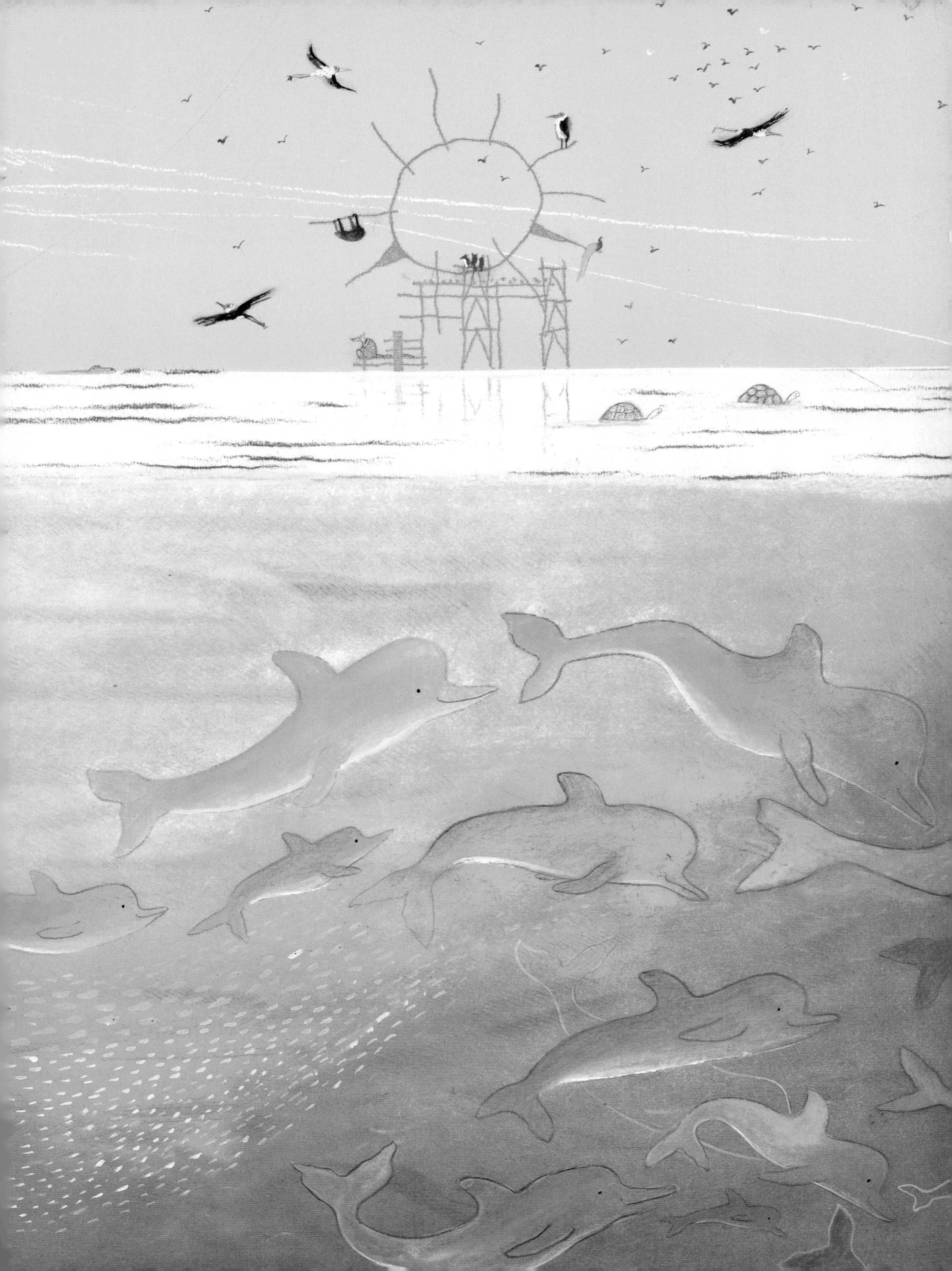

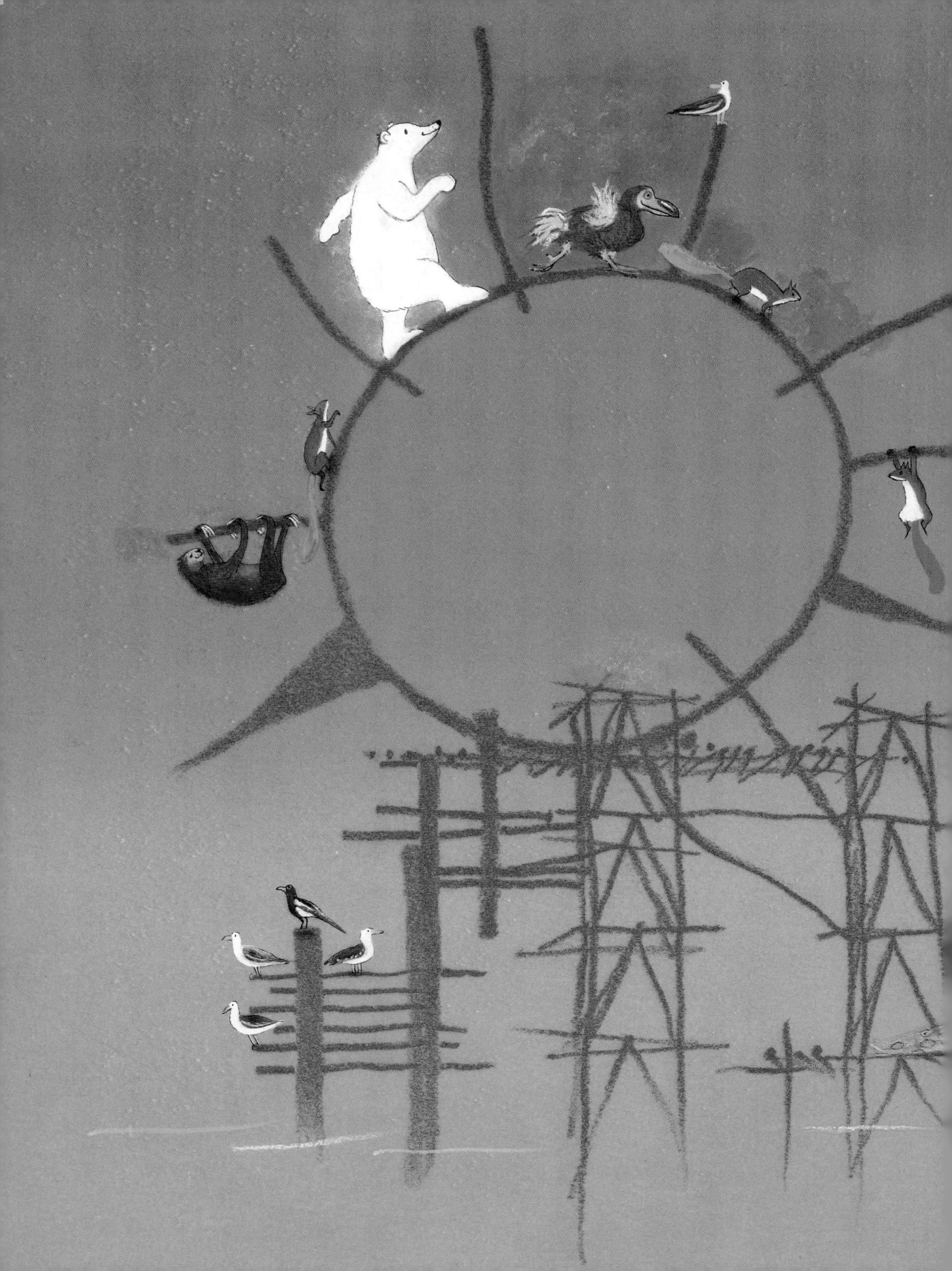

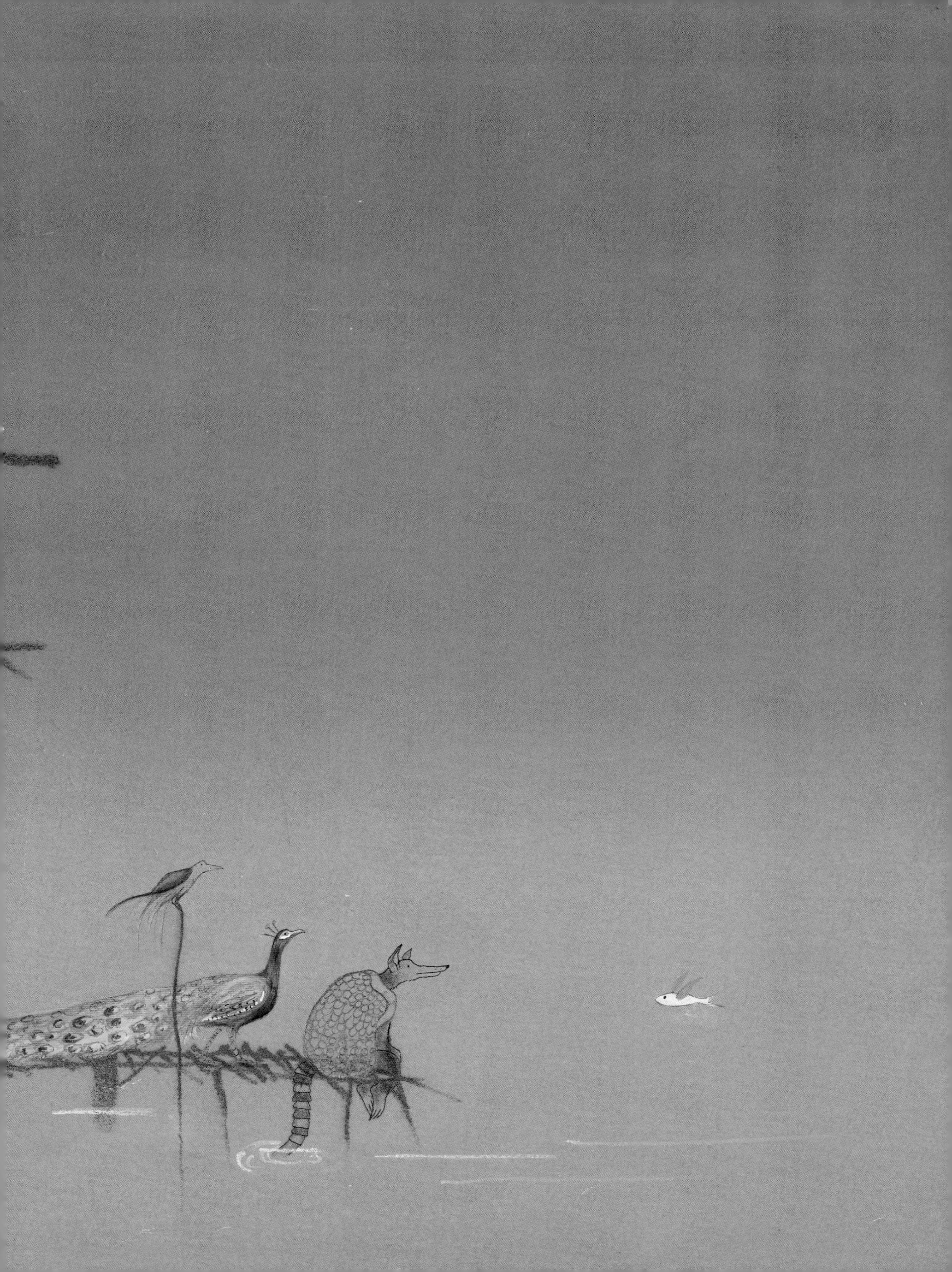

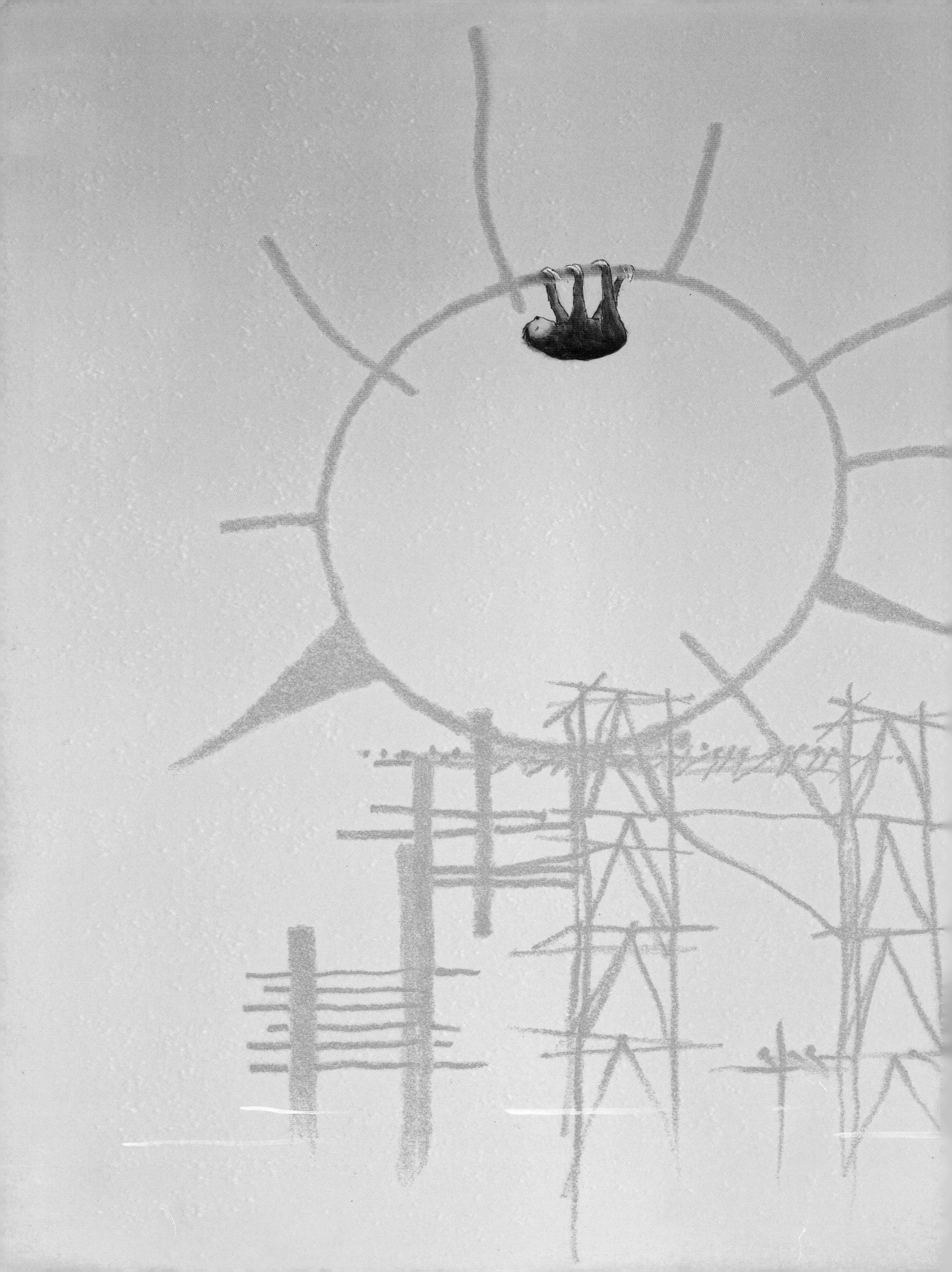

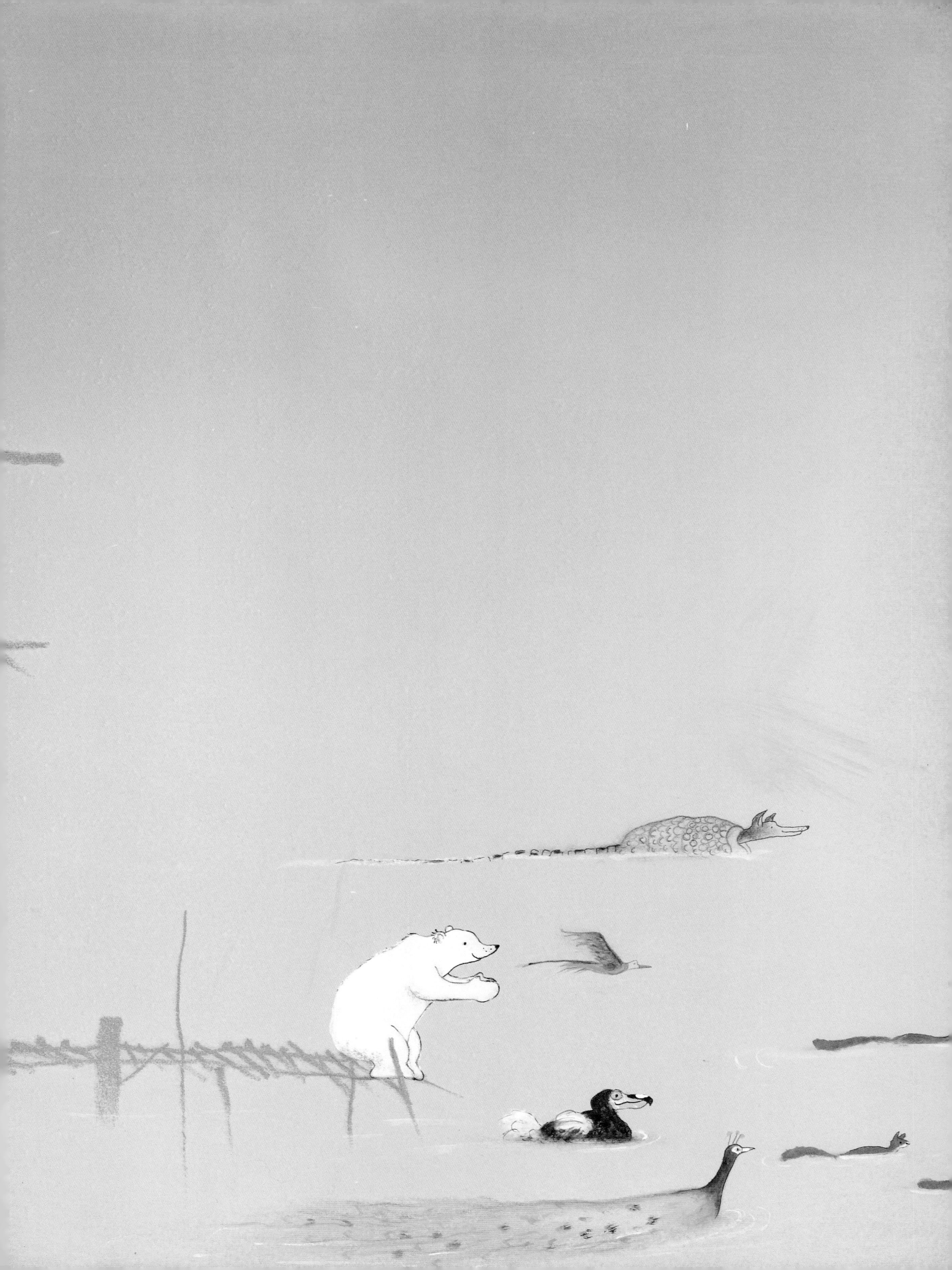

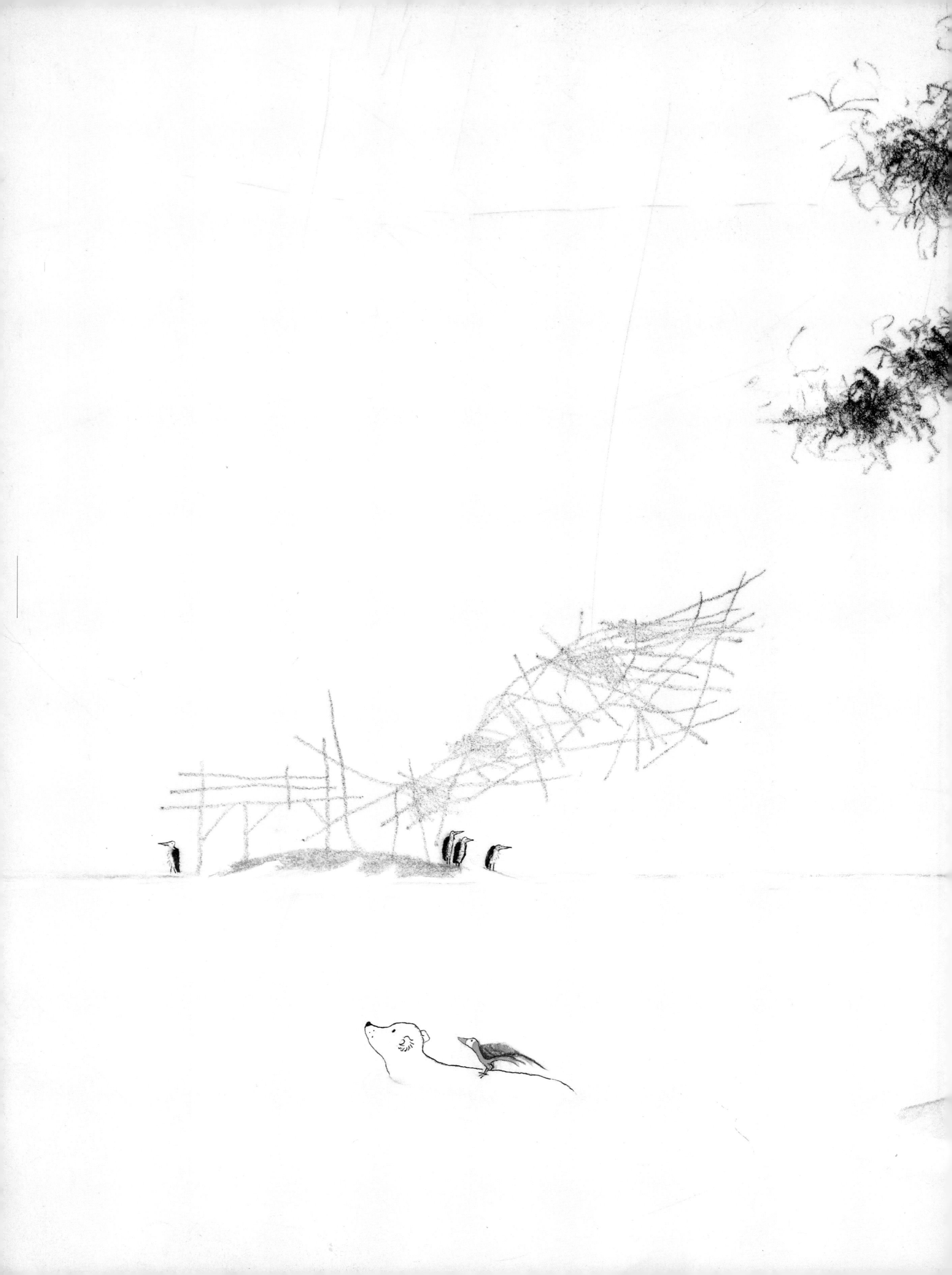

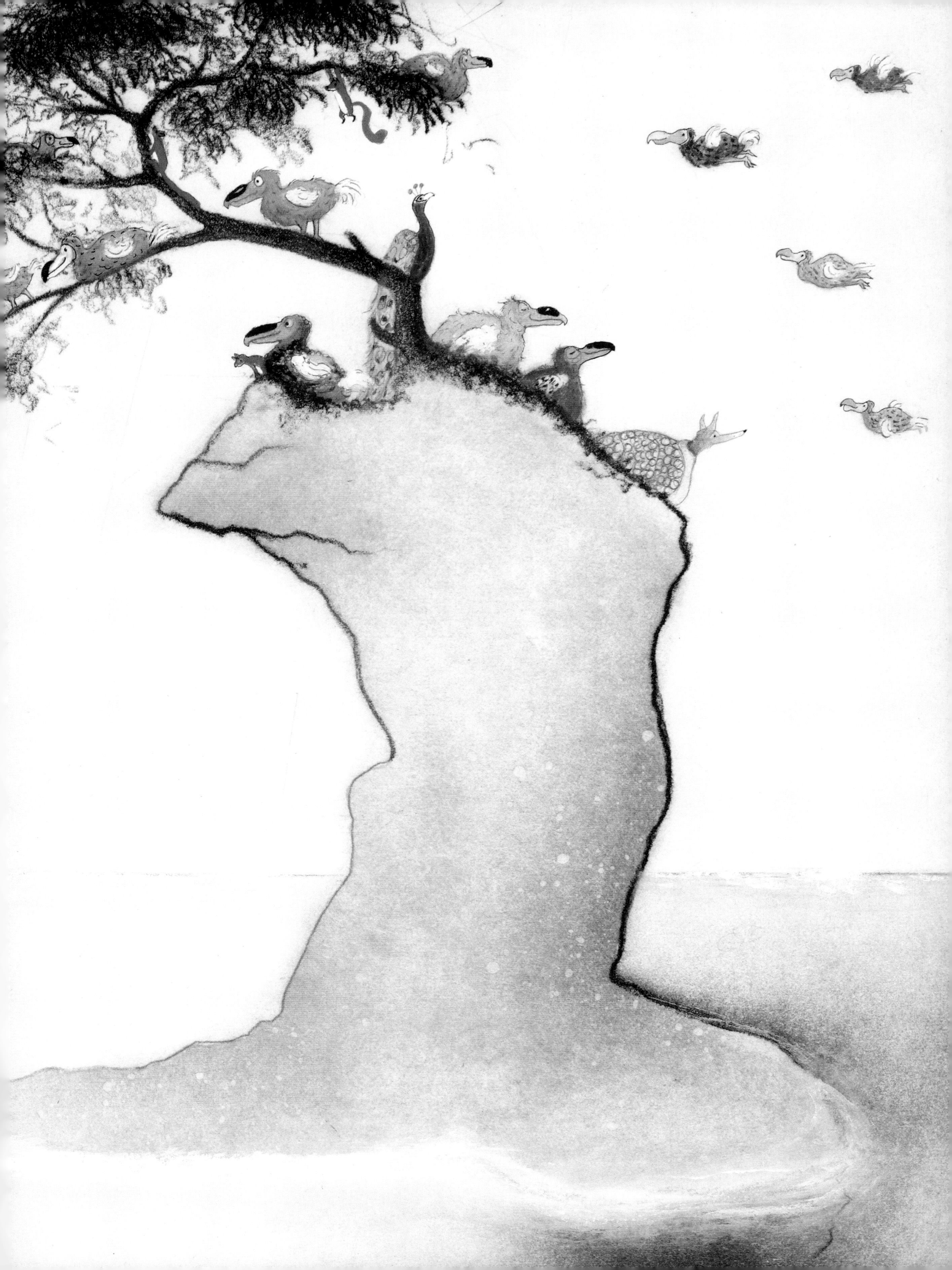

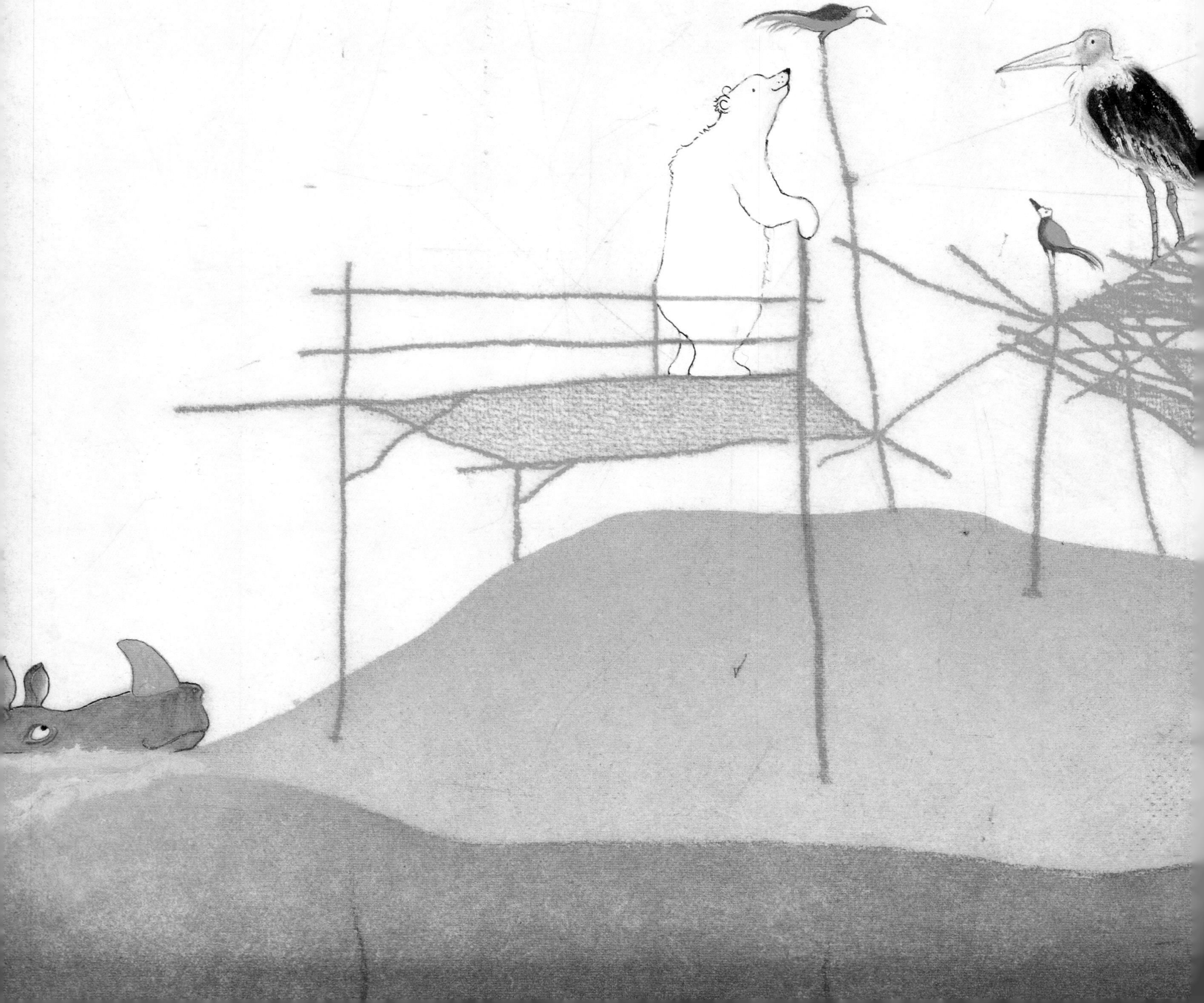

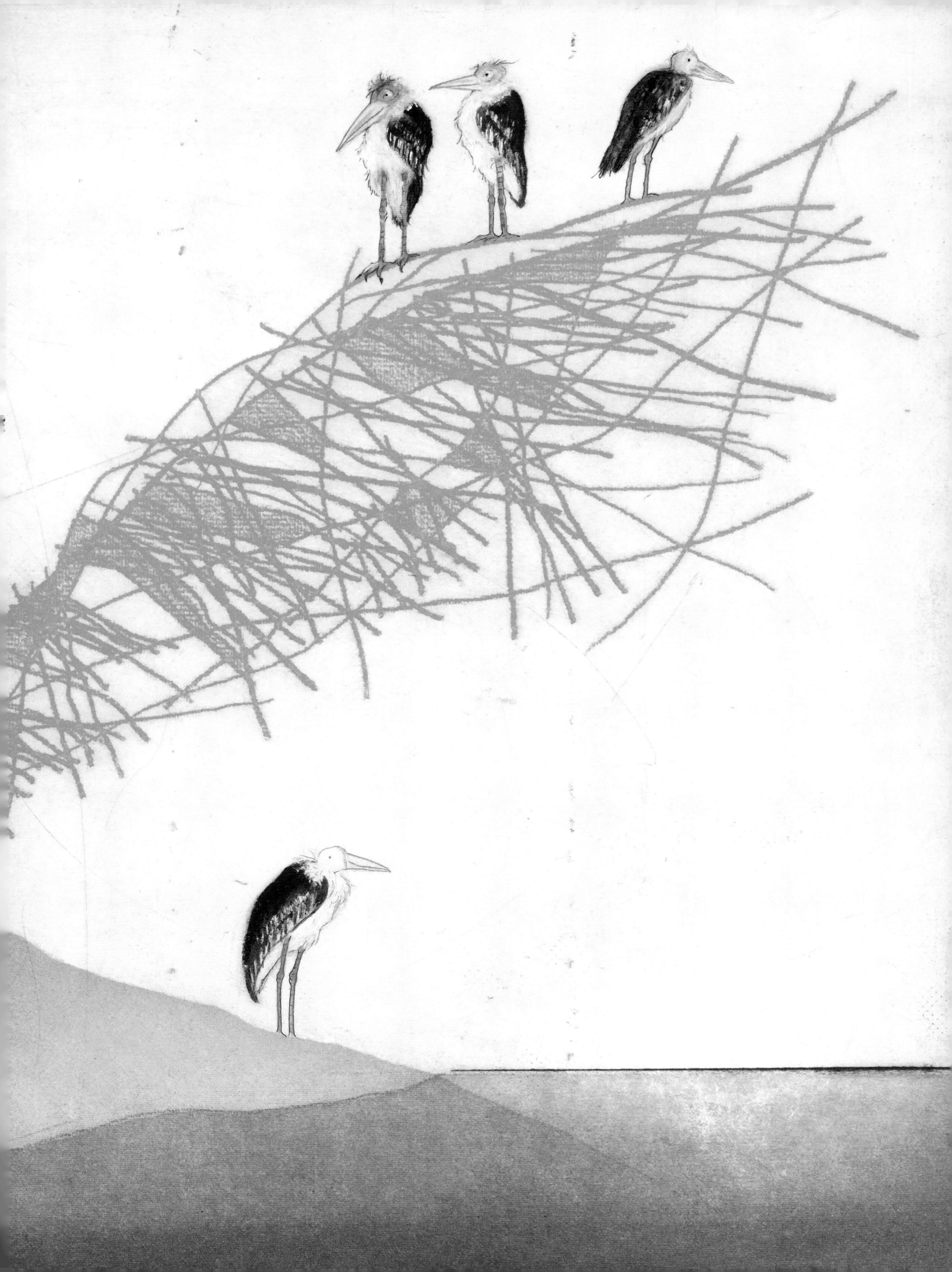

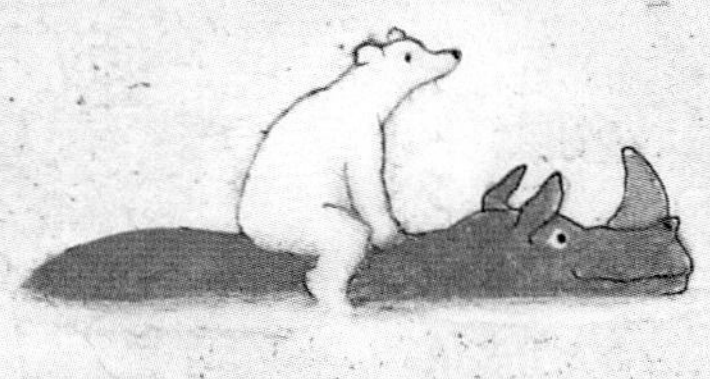

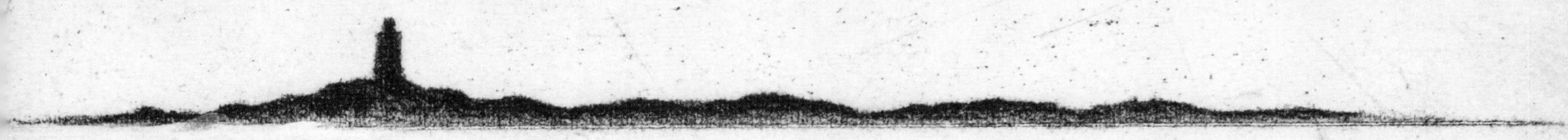

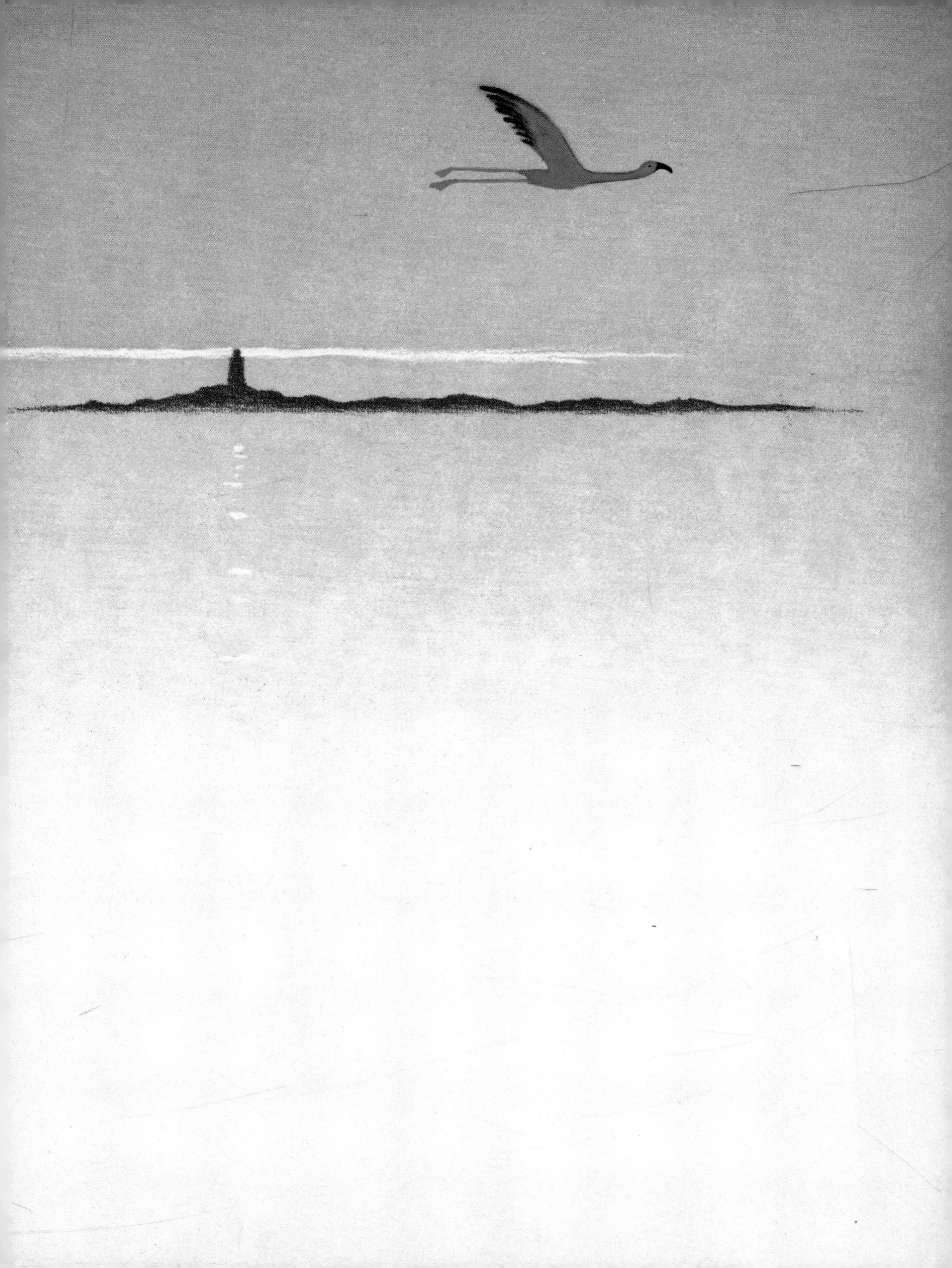

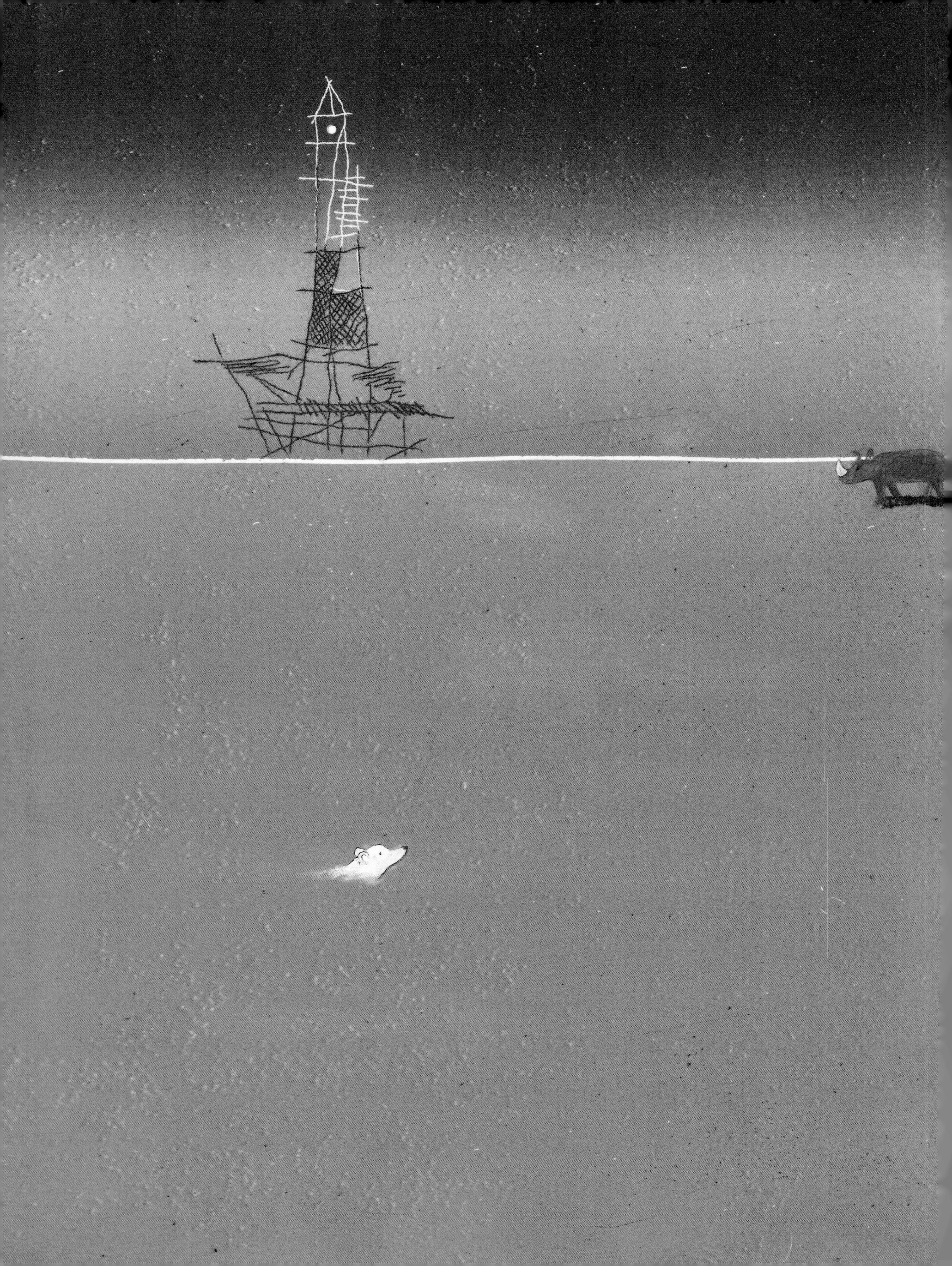

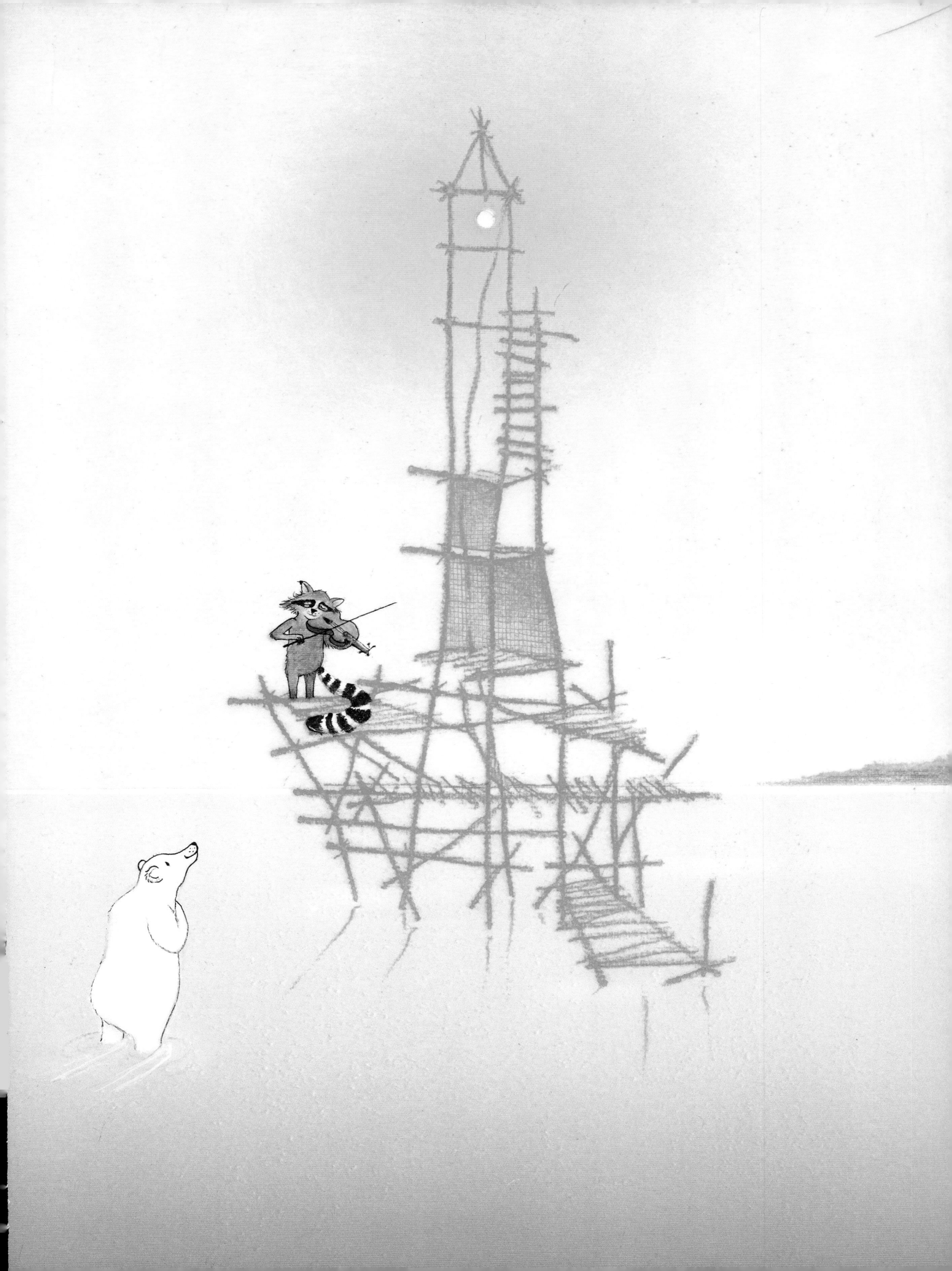

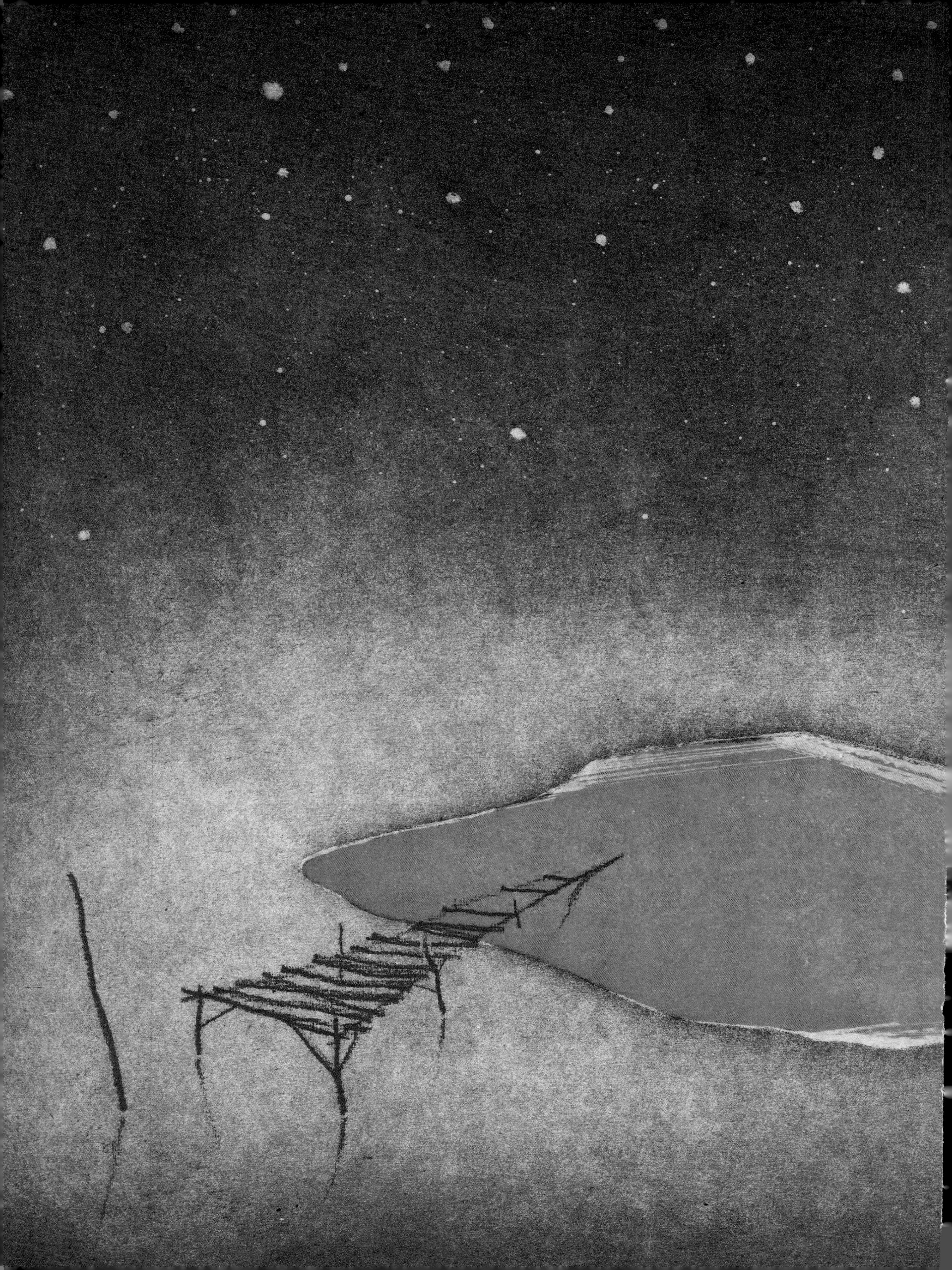

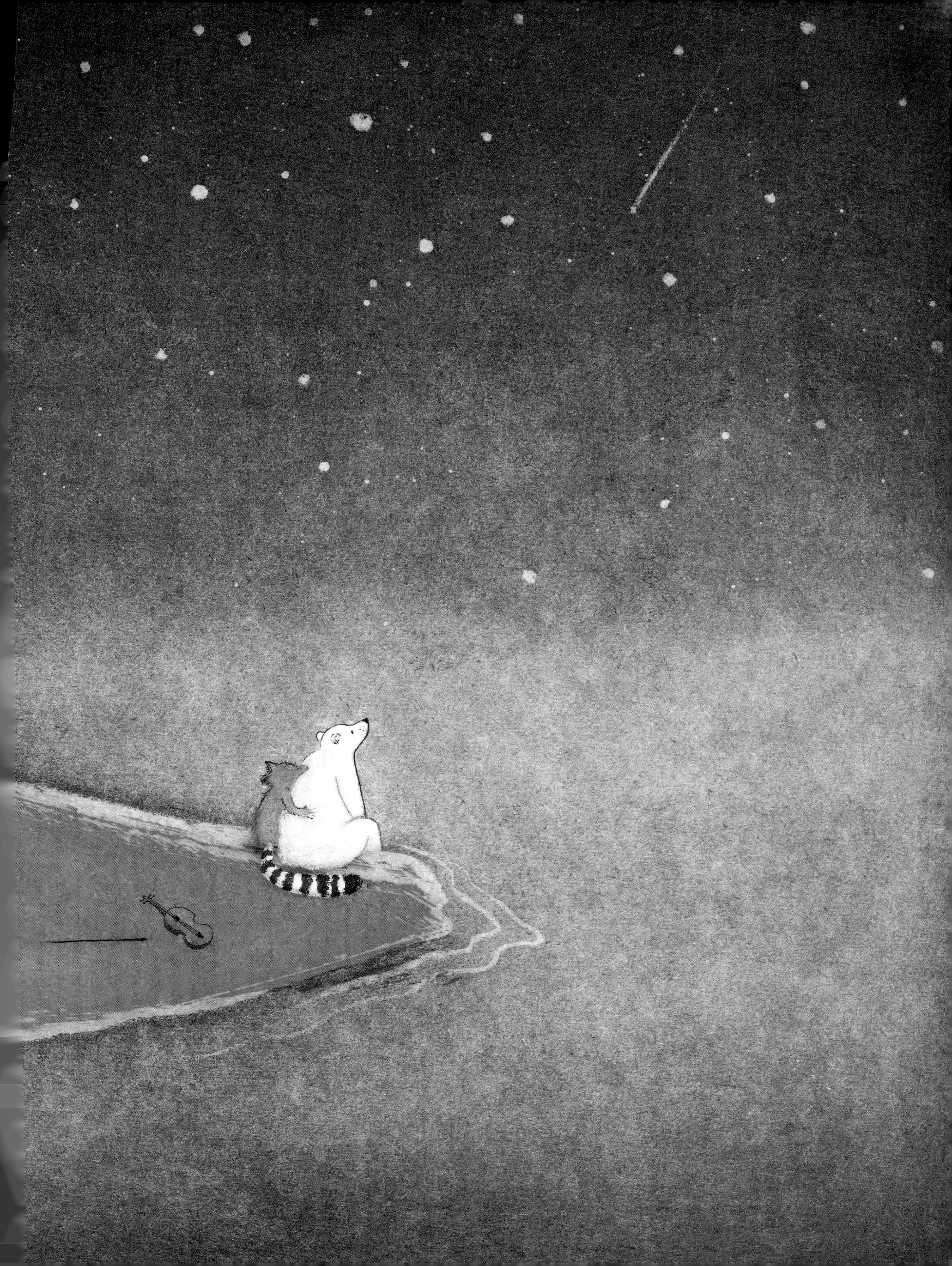

First published in The Netherlands under the title Het eiland